Just Jump Already:

The True Confessions of a Girl becoming a Woman

Onessia Rochell Deshae
Lawson Mosby

This book is dedicated to Momma, Grandma, Granddaddy, my village in the Mississippi Delta, and all the men, women, friends, and family that helped forge me into the beautiful woman I am today.

Foreword

Although this book is fiction, it is grounded in the realisms that many girls experience growing into a young lady and then womanhood. Womanhood is a beautiful, powerful transition in life that should never be taken for granted. Oftentimes, those of us charged with raising young girls into brave women forget to close the gaps of confusion and understanding. Once a young girl, myself, I know how easy it can be to forget what it was like to have so many questions, but very little words to even ask for help, for clarity, for protection, and for direction.

This book serves as a bridge to fill in some of the gaps for many little girls at different phases of their growth.

As their guardians, caretakers, and angels on Earth, we are obligated to guide them until they are almost ready to navigate adult life on their own. There is never a magic number. There is never a special formula. There is never a perfect script to give adults the words to make any conversation about growing up comfortable, but this book can help give adults some starting points. Every day, you are doing your very best, and this book will help you form some of the words and thoughts to express the feelings and fears a parent may not want to speak out loud. However, when we show our children we're human, they will be more likely to open up to the conversations we often pray as parents our girls won't learn the hard way.

As young girls, young ladies, and young women, the world can be a sociable nightmare. Navigating a maze of emotions, facts, and consequences can force any vulnerable person to make simple, life-changing mistakes. Lean on the ones who care for you, whether blood or not, to help you avoid making the same choices again or even for the first time. They are not trying to be bossy or even be in your business; they just want what's best for you because they love you. Give them a chance to give you a chance at living your best life as you jump into womanhood, eyes wide shut. From fitting in, loving herself, understanding puberty, standing up for her values, and so much more, many young girls struggle with finding their voice and the will to say "No", expressing their perspective on topics in their families and social circles, or fighting for what they believe is right/good. Each chapter in this book can help foster healthy conversations for young girls and the adult people in their lives about how to face mental, physical, emotional, or spiritual fear. Furthermore, the questions in the poems can guide these conversations over one or multiple settings. Take your time and use the pieces of this novel that help you help the young girl/teen in your life, even if that person is you, for we can only break the habits that bind us as a family, generation, or culture when we accept that we want something healthier for our children, grandchildren, and others we help along the way.

Chapter 1

"The Peppermint's Prayer"

Levar Burton had just finished my afternoon tutoring session. God's tears were quenching the thirst of the dry Delta earth. Momma was patching the rip in the seat of my favorite shorts. Grandma was slicing the vegetables for Sunday's soup. The sky's belly rumbled. The clouds took a picture of its wonderful landscape. I was happy there was no school tomorrow. I could sleep later, watch cartoons all morning, and play outside all afternoon. Life was perfect. Woof! Woof! Two barks from B.J. always signaled one thing--Granddaddy was home.

He bumped and banged the walls as he called, "Where's my pretty busy, dizzy, missy Izzie? Where's my pretty busy, dizzy, missy Izzie?" B.J.'s tail wagged like that was his name, but the whole house knew that every Friday afternoon like clockwork, Granddaddy clocked out, cashed

his check at the local store, gave Grandma the bill money,

and brought me a bag of sweet treats to enjoy. This Friday

was no different.

BOOM! The sky and clouds grumbled and crackled at

the same time shaking the leaning power lines like a crying

baby. In an instant, the lights were out.

"Unplug 'dat tv from 'da wall, Izzie," Granddaddy

reminded me. In our household, every time there was a

thunderstorm, all the light switches in the house had to be in

the off position, and everything plugged into an outlet had

to be pulled out. We couldn't chance losing the few

appliances, radios, and fans that were in working

condition. As I turned walking back toward the couch,

Granddaddy rattled the brown paper bag I had been waiting for.

"Thank you, Granddaddy," I smiled.

"You're welcome, Baby." Grandad headed to his room to get cleaned for dinner.

In the brown paper bag were ten individually-wrapped peppermint sticks and a ton of penny chewing gum.

The dark clouds blanketed the last brightness of the sky as night came prematurely. The lights were still out. Candles and kerosene lamps were spreading a glow of comfort and a smothering aroma of riding behind a smoking tractor on the highway at turtle speed. Granddaddy must've known my canine company was an early bird, so he brought his dinner into the den where I was. Before he took a bite of his neckbones, he paused.

"Why ain'tchu touched your candy, Izzie?" What's wrong?

I shrugged to spare Granddaddy's feelings.

"Izzie, you hear me? Why ain'tchu touched your candy? You sick or sumthn?"

"No," I whined. They just got all wet, and now the peppermint, all sticky and nasty. Look at'em," I forced the open bag into Granddaddy's face. "They gon' get my hands all sticky, then my clothes gon' get nasty, and Imma get in trouble for messing up my clothes." There must've been a leak in the ceiling right above my eyes because water was passing over my cheekbones down my chin to my neck toward the shore of my shirt collar.

"Ahh, hush up now." Granddaddy's calloused hand consoled my tears as only the hands of a hard-working man could. "I don' toldchu 'bout all 'dat cryin'. Whatchu cryin' 'bout ain't no reason for no pretty girl like you to be fussin' over." Granddaddy wiped his hands on the leg of his overalls. He pulled a peppermint from the brown paper bag, and took my hands. My peas in the pods of his massive hands always seemed to calm my storm. "Izzie, I never told you this, but I think it's time." My tear-filled eyes concentrated on him. "Did you know that the peppermint pray to be loved by little girls and boys. Did you know that?" I shook my head. He continued, "Well, they do. I promise. When I was a little boy, my momma taught me the peppermint prayer, and her daddy taught her the peppermint prayer when she was six-years-old just like you." I don't know if it was because I was six, or if it was because I truly loved and trusted Granddaddy, but the more he talked, the better I felt. He shared with me the peppermint prayer.

Dear God,

I know however you made me is perfect.
Red and white
or green and white,
I have a purpose.
You made me simple.
You made me sweet.
Even when I am broken,
I'm still complete.
Please help me share this happiness
with boys and girls everywhere.
I'm trusting in you, Lord
to hear this peppermint prayer.

My six-year-old wisdom raised its antenna. By the end of Granddaddy's peppermint prayer my sobs were mere whimpers, and the streams coming down my face had evaporated. "Izzie," he lifted my chin with the tip of his finger, "Peppermints are not made to be perfect; they're made to be purposed, to have a purpose--just like you." Granddaddy snapped the melted peppermint in half while it was still in the wrapper. Tiny pieces of peppermint exploded all over the couch. My eyes bucked. "You see, Izzie," Grandaddy chuckled. "Sticky or fresh, old or new, this peppermint just fulfilled its purpose."

Granddaddy wrapped his free arm around me and pulled me closer, and I finished eating the ten sticky peppermint sticks the way God had intended.

****

You are Perfectly Made

You don't have to be perfect,

for you were handmade.

Every eyelash, every finger

every hair in your braid

has a purpose, has a place,

and you should never want to trade

the beautiful, wonderful you that is

perfectly made.

When you were in your mother's belly,

I know that she prayed

for you to just be healthy

with every breath, every bath, and

every time that she laid.

She thanked God for the beautiful, wonderful you

that is perfectly made.

Every day won't be sunshine.

Some days bring the rain.

Every choice you make won't be your best one.

Some of them will have great pain,

but no matter how you face the darkness

face it unafraid,

for you are beautifully, wonderfully, and perfectly made.

Now, don't be mistaken,

mistakes will be made.

Others will think you owe them,

but those debts are man-made

for before you were born

your parents did not take the trade

because they wanted the lovable, beautiful,

wonderful, unmistakable, magnificent,

unstoppable, perfectly purposeful

you.

Chapter 2

"The Spelling Bee"

In nineteen eighty-four, first-grade and Mrs. Stony were not ready for me. Arithmetic flowed like water, but s-p-e-l-l-i-n-g made me sink. Every Monday we got a new word list. Every Friday we took a new test. Twenty words for a seven-year-old drowned all of the oxygen out of me.

F.

That is the grade that poisoned all of my spelling tests each Friday when I brought my graded folder home. No matter how much Momma and Cousin Roger studied with me, I could not make anything above the feared letter grade F. Momma had tried making me write the words ten times each every day. Momma would even write and tape the words around the house so I could see and practice them all day. Momma tried bribing me with a weekly treat, my choice, from the local store if I passed my spelling test. No

matter how much help Momma was giving me, I still could

not p-a-s-s.

By the last Friday in October, Momma threw in the

towel. October twenty-sixth was etched in my

memory. First, because it was Cousin Roger's birthday, and

Cousin Roger was an expert at reminding everyone that his

birthday was always "five days before Halloween." Second,

because this was the F that almost took me out.

I walked in the front room, backpack dragging, head

lowered. Grandma was deep in the "Neighborhood" section

of *The Bolivar Commercial*, but she still heard the defeat in

my stride, so she looked up. "Izzie, how was school

today? How'd tchu do on your tests?" I don't know if the

tears were already hiding in the back of my throat, or if it was the fact that Grandma had just asked about my grades, but before I could even get one word out, I was sobbing relentlessly.

"I-, I go-, I go-, I got an F on my spelling test." The gurgled snot-filled cries poured out of my seven-year-old eyes as Grandma pulled me in her arms on the couch.

"Now, now, Izzie. It's okay. It's okay, y'know. We all done failed at sumthn', even me. I used to be bad at making little girls feel better, but look at me now. I'm practically a pro," she smiled. Grandma smoothed the waves of my tears with every stroke.

I looked up in Grandma's eyes and said, "But Imma fail the first grade, Grandma. I'on wanna fail first grade, Grandma."

"Who- who toldtchu 'dat?" Grandma asked.

"My teacher, Mrs. Stony said that if I keep flunking these spelling tests, Imma fail first grade."

"Well, Mrs. Stony barely know you. She just met you 'dis year. I been knowing you all yo' life, Izrael Katrice Moses, and I know sumthn 'dat Mrs. Stony don't." Grandma's hands squeezed my shoulder as if she were transferring some of her energy into me. "Mrs. Stony don't know that you is a Moses, and Moses just like water--we have a perfect memory. And since you made of mostly water, you a natural-born speller. Y'know 'dat, Izzie?"

"Ugh, ugh." I was not convinced.

Grandma continued, "And since I seems like da only one who can do anythang right 'round here lately, Imma teach you how to be a master speller and reader."

Grandma and Granddaddy had shared the stories many times with me about how Grandma only finished sixth grade, and Granddaddy only finished second, but with my seven-year-old wisdom and my super math skills, I knew six was more than one, so Grandma was my last shot at passing the first grade. "What we gon' do?" I asked.

"The first thang we gon' do is teach you how to spell your first word. Water. W-A-T-E-R. Water. Say it. Spell it. Say it, Izzie."

"But Grandma," I interjected, "water ain't on my spelling list."

"'Dat's okay. Imma teach you a trick 'dat I bet even Mrs. Stony don't know." Grandma told me that to have a memory like water, you have to see the word you want to spell because water always sees every hole in everything that blocks its path. No matter how big, strong, or tall it is, water will always find its way through any obstacle. She told me that's what I have to do to be a master speller, see every inch of the words. "Pull out 'dat spelling test you jus' failed."

Grandma began describing and talking to me about the ins and outs, the looks and actions, and he curves and lines of every single word. By sunset, I had spelled every word correctly from the last spelling test. Grandma signed all of my graded work in my folder, and I spent the rest of the weekend carefree.

Monday morning, Mrs. Stony reached my desk. "Izrael, did you get your work signed?"

"Yes, Ma'am," I said, handing her my folder. Mrs. Stony opened my folder to verify the signatures.

"What's this?" She pointed at the two words penned by the red F at the top of last week's spelling test. She knew I couldn't read. Heck, I could barely spell. Why would Mrs. Stony ask me what those two words were?

"I- I don't know," I answered.

"It says, "Forever Growing.","" Mrs. Stony read, teeth clenched. "Hmph." Mrs. Stony's nose wrinkled in a million places. She turned around as if in a hurry, and continued collecting students' folders.

I did not see Grandma write those words. Grandma did not confess to it either, but every afternoon after school, Grandma would pull me beside her on the couch, and we would study my weekly words. Every Friday from that day forward, the spelling tests that were trying to take me under were a thing of the past. Mrs. Stony and all of my classmates noticed my spelling was improving dramatically.

November second, November ninth, and November sixteenth came and left, and each time an A graced the top of my spelling test. I was on cloud n-i-n-e.

Because of Grandma and my water-like memory, my A-streak continued the rest of the school year. And thanks to Grandma, I became my school's nineteen eighty-five spelling bee champion, and I've been a super speller ever since.

My first-grade year, when I was drowning in an ocean of failure, I was blessed that Grandma became my o-x-y-g-e-n, and she was only in the sixth grade.

****

Champions Takes Time

They say it takes a village to raise a child,

but sometimes it just takes one.

One person, one minute, one woman, one man

to show some attention.

Some people may say girls rule this whole world.

Just know they didn't get that strong on their own.

Strong mind, strong will, strong faith, strong love

for yourself and all your milestones.

They say it's not about how fast you reach your goals;

it's more about the fact that you continue the incline

because champions are not born overnight, my dear.

True champions take time.

They say live life without excuses.

Give every moment your best shot.

Shoot for the moon, the promotion, the part, the dream

whether it happens on the first try or not.

Some say do what makes you happy

even it takes a while,

so while you wait, you work, you pray, you learn, you slay

until that inch turns into a mile

They say it's not about how fast you reach your goals;

it's more about the fact that you continue the incline

because champions are not born overnight, my dear.

True champions take time.

Chapter 3

"The Fight"

"Friday. After school. We fightin'."

The flight of me swinging was reduced to a slow rock with two words--*We fightin'?* "What did I do to you?"

"Izrael, you ain' do nothin'. I jus' don't like you. Sooo, we fightin' on Friday. Meet me at the corner. hmph. Iz-ra-el? What kind of name is that for a girl anyway?" Leviatha stomped away with her new crew snickering behind.

When I looked at my size compared to Leviatha's, we were close in height, but not in weight. *Can a skinny girl punch as hard as someone with a little more muscle?* All day I contemplated ways to approach Leviatha. Ways to make eye contact, hoping to get a glimpse of humanity or kindness in her eyes, but she wouldn't look my way. Until the end of the day.

RIIIIIING!

I shoved my tablets, books, and pencils into my backpack trying to beat the goons out the door to walk home. As soon as I reached the exit closest to the rock road,

"HEY!" Leviatha snaps at me as we collide trying to leave through the same door. Her library books crash to the floor. "You betta watch wher' you goin', girl."

My eyes connected with her, and that's when I saw it. Nothing. One second of eye contact told me that Leviatha didn't like me. Leviatha wanted to show me and the rest of the world that she didn't like me either. The space between her top lids and bottom lids were the color of a winter storm raging in the dark of the night. After meeting Fear for the first time in a girl who looked like me, I was confused.

Did I say something wrong?

Why does she not like me?

Did someone lie on me?

Is she jealous of me?

Why does she want to fight me?

Will she change her mind?

Should I tell my grandma?

Will Grandma get mad at me if I fight back?

Should I turn the other cheek?

Should I fake sick?

Should I fight back?

Should I ask my cousin to help me?

Do I even have a chance of beating her?

If I fight her, will she leave me alone after that?

Should I just avoid her every day?

On Tuesday, I took Washington street to go home. On Wednesday, I tried the Main Street route to get home. On Thursday, I attempted to take Park Ave. to get home. No matter which way I went, I still had to cross paths with Leviatha because her house was on the street directly behind mine. Either way, she would find me.

Friday. 2:45 P.M. The final bell rings. I scurried out the door hoping to miss Fear at the corner. For a second, I even thought I saw Mrs. Malloy slow down on her way out the parking lot. I'm not sure, though, because I walked with my eyes focused on my feet. *Walk faster. Walk faster. Walk faster. Walk faster.* But my feet were being

stubborn. My cousin walked behind me. Crowds of fellow

walkers swarmed around me. Fear stood before me. I had

no choice but to fight. My hands were cemented in the

pockets of my khaki shorts. My shoes had been replaced

with boulders. My guts had been replaced with the nerves

of a butterfly. *What do I do? Do I drop my book bag? Do*

I try to reason with her? Do I cry? Do I run? Do I swing

first? If I swing first, will I get in trouble when I get

home? Do I pick up a rock and use--

BAM! Leviatha's fist shook every thought in my

brain with one firm swing. My thoughts rattled like pennies

in a tin can. I had been knocked into next week. It was

over. The crowd dispersed with mumbles of commentary

from the corner. The silence between my cousin and I on

the walk home revealed the victor. Walking in the front room was different that day. I veiled my defeat behind the shoulders of my cousin as we crossed the threshold.

"Hey, Grandma."

"Hey, Babies. How was your d-- Izrael, what happened to your eye?"

"i-i got into a fight today."

"with who?"

"with Fear."

"Oh?...Now, go wash your hands and get to 'dat dining room table and start on yo' homework."

"Yes, Ma'am."

"I'll bring you some ice to soothe 'dat eye." But I didn't need ice. What I needed, Grandma wasn't ready to give.

****

The Lesson

What are you afraid of?

What keeps your soul mute?

What keeps you running?

What pollutes your mind and heart until you don't recognize

the face you see in the mirror?

What people can protect you?

What place can you go

to hide all your insecurities?

What shadows lurk in the words and habits that make you

afraid of who you are becoming?

What lies do you tell you?

What mental blankets keep you safe

until you are smothering with

whatever craziness invades your peace and replaces it with

doubt?

What is your exit plan?

What are your next steps

when the voices tell you it's okay?

What's okay about being afraid to speak up for yourself

despite the labels you've been bathed with since birth?

What weighs on your heart like lead?

What clouds your mind?

What scars from fear

do you want to leave behind?

What other seeds are you watering when you don't talk

about your fears?

Chapter 4

"The Music Teacher"

There were sixty-nine students, one principal, and nine teachers. I was only nine years old, but I will remember this teacher until I am eight hundred and eighty-- Mrs. Patricia Malloy. Her hair was a mix of beach sand, Delta dirt, and corn at harvest time. Her curls were the size of sidewalk chalk. Her eyes were always moving as if she never slept. Her hands were soft and inviting. Her voice was the envy of angels. Her smile, a reflection of her heart.

It was the week before Christmas break, and the entire school was diligently working to prepare for the school's annual Christmas program and weekly classroom festivities. I was the last student to walk in class. It was expected.

"Thank you, Izrael."

"You're welcome, Mrs. Malloy." I placed her Diet Rite on the corner of her desk, my snowman fingerprints searching for the warmth of my jeans.

Mrs. Malloy knew we were ready for the five songs we had to perform in the program, so she began music class with an intro that none of us expected.

"Good morning, songbirds."

"Good morning, Mrs. Malloy."

"There will be no Christmas melody drills today, but I have one last lesson I would like to share with you all because I know my smart, mature songbirds can understand the message and share it with those you love. I want to teach you a special song. Christmas is just around the corner, and I know many of you will return to us after the break ready to share everything Santa brought you. I can't wait, but the song we will learn today will help you at Christmas, after Christmas, really, anytime you are faced with something that feels big and scary. Have you ever been faced with something or someone that seemed big and scary?"

"Yes," we shook our heads.

"Well, me, too, but the story I will use to help you understand the message of today's song is the story of Caleb the spy. Raise your hands high if you've ever heard the Bible story of David and Goliath?"

Thirty twinkling fingers shot in the air.

"Noah and the ark?"

Our hands stayed high.

"What about Caleb the spy?"

The space above our heads our hands had occupied became a ghost town. Mrs. Malloy had gotten our attention. With our eyes on her, she began telling the story of how Caleb was one of the twelve spies that Moses and Aaron sent to check out the land of Canaan. Moses wanted them to report back to him on how the land and food was, how the people were, and any details on how the children of Israel would be able to conquer the people and possess the land that God has promised them. After the spies told Moses that the land was filled with milk, honey, and the best tasting fruit, Moses directed the men to get ready to go to Canaan to take the land. As soon as most of the spies heard Moses' decision, they began to show fear. One spy explained how they would never be able to defeat the people in the land of Canaan because the Canaanites were men of great stature--giants, and the Israelites were mere grasshoppers compared to the Canaanites. Every spy shared this same hesitation, everyone except Caleb. Caleb pleaded to Moses and Aaron to go take the land. Go into the land of Canaan and possess it without fear, for if God brought them to this land, God will give them this land, too.

Mrs. Malloy was sharing an underdog from the Bible, and with this underdog story, Mrs. Malloy hooked us. "Now, I know you all are strong eight and nine-year olds, but even strong songbirds like you will encounter a giant in life someday, and when you do have to face that giant, I want you to remember these words..."

Mrs. Malloy's magical fingers began to pump out Bing Crosby's melody, "You've gotta ac-cent-tuate the positive. E-lim-minate the negative. Latch-on to the

affirmative. Don't mess with Mr. In-between..." Mrs.

Malloy sang this song for us all the way through one time

first. Then, she paused. "How can the words to this song

help you face your fears--your giants? Tony? Mrs. Malloy

called on the tiny, fragile boy in our class who hardly

spoke. Tony, how do you think the words to this song can

help you face your giants?"

Tony stared into the emptiness beyond Mrs. Malloy's

bright eyes and whispered, "You don't fight the hands that

feed you."

"Wha-- What was that, Tony? Speak up a little. We

can't hear you."

"N-neva mind." Tony shrugged his shoulders and

pulled at the hems of his sleeves. It was not odd that Mrs.

Malloy called on Tony to talk because she always called on all of us, but it was strange when she moved him to be right beside her on the risers. It was even stranger that two weeks ago, she began keeping him after class every day. It was weird that she brought an extra lunch bag to class for the past month. It was different when Mrs. Malloy began paying extra special attention to Tony.

Could she--? Did she kno--? How did she find out that--? My curiosity made me wonder if Mrs. Malloy had figured out why Tony was so quiet. The other teachers did not seem to care that Tony wore the same plaid shirt half of the week. The other teachers did not bring Tony cream to rub on the bruises on his neck, arms, and head. The other teachers did not see how skinny Tony had gotten since the start of the school year. The other teachers learned to not call on Tony to talk in class. They just let him disappear into the walls of the classrooms.

After we finished learning the song, Mrs. Malloy stood behind her piano and said, "As some of you go home home to your giants over the Christmas break, remember that giants can't grow anymore, but you, oh you, my songbirds are still growing stronger and stronger each day, and one day you will be taller, braver, smarter, and much stronger than those giants. When you realize that, your giants won't be able to hurt you anymore." Even though Mrs. Malloy's voice projected this message to the entire class, her eyes were fixed on Tony. She continued, "Until you can face your giants, remember, my sweet songbirds, you are not alone."

Tony did not return to school after Christmas break. The other teachers did not notice his absence. The other teachers kept accidentally calling his name on the roll for weeks. However, our first day back in Mrs. Malloy's room, she smiled as if she knew exactly where Tony had gone. At the beginning of this first music class after the break, Mrs. Malloy locked eyes with me, and said, "Izrael, can you move to Tony's old spot on the risers? He won't be needing it anymore. He's been promoted for facing his giants." I shuffled to my new spot by Mrs. Malloy, and prepared to sing my heart out.

****

The Little Things

Did you notice I haven't smiled today?

Did you see the bags under my eyes?

I've been crying all night,

and I don't know why?

My emotions are hard to disguise.

Did you notice I haven't bathed in a week?

Do you smell depression's tears?

I've hardly spoken two words all month,

and my classmates are just my peers.

What are the signs when I'm screaming for help?

When do I want you to step in?

Would you even know where to start,

Or would you pray for it all to end?

I know sometimes it's hard being a parent,

but what's it like to be your child?

Did you notice how long it took me to wake up this

morning?

I haven't done that in a while.

Did you notice that I got an A on my test,

or do the F's only get "the talk"?

It's the little things that matter to me

like going for a random afternoon walk.

How big do the bruises of my youth have to be

for you to listen to my heart?

Why do our conversations cause pomp and circumstance

and push us further apart?

It's the little things that matter to me

because my heart is still so very small.

It's the little things that matter for me

when between us we've built a huge wall.

My favorite color, my favorite drink,

what type of music makes me smile?

Did you notice that even though I'm growing up,

I always still want to be your sweet, little child?

Chapter 5

"Show Me Your Scars"

Today, my aunt moved back in our house with her three boys. I didn't know exactly why, and every night Aunt Aretha, Livia, Benita, and Grandma would sit in the living room discussing the whys. And as eight-year-old, I had to stay in a child's place.

"Izrael, go back down 'dat hall."

I sauntered towards my room using the walls as speed bumps.

"Chile, he ain't worth it," Aunt Benita said. "Ain't no man worth it."

"Shol ain't," Aunt Aretha agreed. "You can do bad all by yosef. Ya see me, don't ya? I been divorced from 'dat sorry-excuse-for-a-man for ten years now, and I'm perfectly fine."

From the rise and fall of the sounds of the storms in their voices I could tell from the safety of my room that the topic they were discussing was related to a man—one who had just been thrown overboard without a life jacket.

For the next month, Aunt Livia and her three boys were in rehab in our home. She didn't say much around us, but I could tell from her actions alone that her heart had been broken—again. At night I could hear the whimpers and weeping that Livia's walls sang. She camouflaged her pain by staying busy. Every day she scrubbed the bathroom toilet. Every day she shined the tub. Every day she pierced the air with Lysol. Every day she glossed the linoleum with Mop n' Glo. And she did this everyday while blasting her music therapy—Mississippi Mass Choir.

Aunt Livia was hurting. Her heart had been torn open, and she was bleeding uncontrollably, but coming home had applied just enough pressure to her arteries to stop the bleeding. By the end of their second month's reprieve at our house, Aunt Livia and her boys were ready to move to their next destination. I could feel that Aunt Livia wasn't ready to go, but she refused to let a little open heart surgery slow her down.

Show me your scars? I wanted to ask her as Aunt Livia and my three cousins were packing boxes and other belongings in our family's cars, vans, and truck, helping her move.

show me your scars. I wanted to plea as my Aunt introduced us to her new heart doctor. He was moving in with Aunt Livia and her boys to help her heal from her open heart surgery in their new home 35 miles away.

SHOW ME YOUR SCARS! I wanted to scream to Aunt Livia as she and her new heart doctor discussed with joy her healing therapy schedule and treatments.

I tugged at the hem of Aunt Livia's blouse as she was walking out the screen door.

"What is it, Izrael? You gon' miss me? I know it. Imma miss you, too, But I'm not far. You'll see me almost every week."

"Show me your scars?" I whispered.

"What? Whatcha say? I can't hear you, Izzie. Speak up. Wha-, Whatcha say?" Aunt Livia's bellow had gotten the attention of every other human within a 5-mile radius, and now all eyes were on me.

"N- never mind. It's nothin'," I cowered.

Aunt Livia and her three boys moved on to the next phase of their lives, and I never knew how she got those scars.

By the time I turned eighteen, Aunt Livia had had 3 more open-heart surgeries and so many scars that not even an elephant-sized bandage could cover them all. At this point, I think Aunt Livia knew this fact, too. So she wore them proudly everywhere she went. She had no choice. Now that I was older, the "stay-in-a-child's-place" adage didn't work as much anymore. I was able to sit-in on more adult conversations with my aunts and Grandma. However, every time the subject came up about one of Aunt Livia's, Aunt Benita's, or Aunt Aretha's scars, they would all change the subject.

"Chile, you know ion got no health insurance."

Once that sentence was said,

POOF! Just like magic, the subject about men was changed.

I was just starting to date boys, and they would begin to redirect their conversations to me or one of my other girl cousins who was present. I would often walk away from my aunts' living-room conversations more confused about how to interact with boys than I did from talking about dating and boys with my school friends. One day, when my Aunt Livia realized I was interested in seriously dating one guy, she pulled me to the side after church.

"Izzie, protect your heart."

I looked at her with a raised brow. "What?"

"Look, Izzie," she said, "I know you watched me get my heart broken time after time after time, and I didn't have health insurance."

"Ohhhhhk?"

"I can tell you're getting serious about Jordan, and I don't want you to end up with the scars I have. Just be careful and protect your heart." Jordan is a nice boy, but ya'll are still so young. Take your time," she cautioned.

Aunt Livia walked away without waiting for me to reply and interlocked arms with her fifth heart doctor in ten years. From the way they waltzed out of the church doors, I could tell his therapy was helping her heal.

****

The Birds and the Bees

Hey, you?

Yes, you.

How do you expect me to learn from your mistakes

if you bury them under two-hundred pounds of concrete?

Hey, you?

Yes, you.

How can I ever know how to create healthy relationships

if you only go to the doctor when you are sick?

Whenever you talk to me about birds,

you just mention how annoying their songs are.

Whenever you talk to me about bees,

You merely focus on their sting.

Did you forget how the bees pollinate the heart of our

survival?

Shouldn't a young girl know?

Shouldn't a young girl be in the know?

Hey, you?

Yes, you.

Don't forget that one day this young girl's trunk will spread

like the oaks,

her limbs will move with the wind,

her lips will whisper spell-bound enchantments that even the

gods can't ignore,

her roots will birth many nations.

Don't forget to tell me how the birds' melodies can confuse

an educated fool.

Hey, you?

Yes, you.

Just talk to me about loving myself first

before the world consumes me with the

idea that I have to run to someone else's love

to feel important.

Hey, you?

Don't forget to remind me every day that

the bees don't need the birds' help to pollinate the world.

Chapter 6

"When Apple Trees Bloom"

My skin is brown. My legs are long. My hair is full. My backbone is yellow. My book sense measures that of a 6th grader, my street sense, a newborn. I'm a girl.

I awoke to the sounds of bacon searing, eggs scrambling, and grits popping. Grandma always made sure we had at least one hot breakfast a week during the school year, and summertime was no different. My nails were polished. My feet outside-ready. My teeth were brushed. My stomach was turning somersaults in the middle of a lightning storm. I'm a girl.

I sat down beside Grandma after breakfast in her favorite spot at the corner of the sofa.

"You ready to walk to the post office with me?" Grandma asked.

"Yes, Ma'am."

"Go throw on your shoes, so we can go."

"Yes, Ma'am."

We walked down Numbers Street towards the post office. The strays escorted us every step of the way. Grandma was holding my hand. We shared a glance. She gave me a wink. I knew what time it was. I scanned our surroundings to search for my first question. Grandma guided me.

"Grandma, why is the sky blue?"

"It's blue because blue is the color of trust. God wanted the birds to trust his direction when they fly, so he keeps the sky nice, pretty, and blue to help direct their flight and vision."

Grandma, why is the sun so bright?"

"The sun shines so bright because that's God's way of sharing happiness with us. When the sun shines bright on you, we get vitamin D, and vitamin D is good for our teeth, and when we have enough vitamin D, our smiles will always be as bright as the sun.

Grandma, why do dogs have to walk on four legs?

"Oh, that's an easy one," Grandma bragged. "It's an honor for dogs to walk on four legs because they are forever thankful to God for creating them. So every second of every day, dogs pray. When they bark, they are singing songs of worship and praise." Grandma squeezed my hand a little tighter. We shared another glance. Izrael, we could learn a lot from dogs about prayer and worship. Y'know it?"

"Yes, Ma'am."

We reached the post office in five questions. We made it back home in six. By the time we got home, my stomach was practicing Jiu jitsu. Stomach pains for an eleven-year-old were usually soothed with the pink stuff, but before I could tell Grandma that my stomach was hurting, I felt like I had to go to the bathroom.

I pulled down my shorts and underwear. I sat on the toilet. And that's when I saw it. A pool of crimson tide was in the seat of my underwear. I had seen it on tv. I had overheard classmates whisper about it from time to time, but I was not prepared for this new side of being a girl.

I could not blink. I could not talk. I did not want to breathe, for every breath caused me to flood. I thought I was dying. I had the blood trail to prove it.

"Izrael, what's takin' you so long in 'dat bathroom?" Grandma's question aroused me from my toilet coma. "IZ-ZIE, WHAT CHU DOIN' IN DAYR?"

For years Grandma and I had played the questions game. Sometimes I would ask her questions; sometimes she would ask me, but never did she ask me any questions about what was happening to me now.

What do I say to her? Will I get in trouble for messing up my clothes? What's happening to me? How long will this happen to me? Will I get sicker? What do I do? What do I do? Will I still be able to turn cartwheels with my friends? How can I sit down and stand up like I used to? Why does this happen to girls? Why do I have to be a gir-?

"IiiiZIEEEE," Grandma rings from the front room.

"Ma'am?"

"Are you alright in dayr?"

"N-, no, Ma'am. Grandma," I bubbled, "something's wrong with me. I messed up my clothes. There's...there's blood in my panties. I'm bleeding, Grandma. What do I do?" This was the first time Grandma and I played the questions game at the house. The questions game was meant to be played on a long drive, trip, or walk to help pass the time, but today, all I wished is that time could move like lightning through my life and make me leave this moment, this new part of being a girl behind--so far behind that I'd need *Atlantis* to feel this way, be this way again.

"Izzie?" Grandma called as if she were ready to give me an answer to my new silent questions.

"Yes, Ma'am." I knew if anybody had an answer to this monster, Grandma would.

"Go to your room. Grab a clean pair of underwear. Look under the bathroom counter and grab the blue plastic bag with those pads innit. Take one out. Peel the stickers off. Stick the pad in your underwear."

I followed Grandma's directions to the letter because I had very little knowledge of what was happening to my body. Every part of my existence wanted to crawl under the floorboards and sleep until God did his thang. Who was I kiddin'?

I eventually took my place back beside Grandma on the couch in the front room; I was not in the mood for any more questions. I didn't even know what questions to ask. Grandma squeezed my hand. We shared a glance. We sat in silence.

My skin is brown. My legs are long. My hair is full. My head is pounding. My feet are shaking. My nails are polished. My backbone is yellow. My hands are soft. My stomach is tumbling. My eyes are closed. My mind is drowning. My ears are pierced. My insides are leaking. I'm a girl--a girl with no blueprint on how to be a woman in a girl's body--

but I wish I was a boy.

****

The Evolution of a Young Lady

I'm not a doctor.

I'm not a pro.

I'm just a parent,

and I want you to know

that we all are human;

we all bleed,

but girls are stronger.

You hold the seeds

to all of our futures.

It's kept safely in your womb,

but it doesn't happen overnight.

Your body has to make room

to grow into its power.

I know this may sound strange,

but little girls' bodies have to grow.

Your body has to change.

Between the ages of eight to thirteen,

your little girl looks will bloom

like a flower. You start to get more compliments.

You start to wear perfume.

On the inside your body's also changing

more than the eyes can see.

This change only happens to girls.

It's your evolution to being a lady.

This change will bring some discomfort;

it will often bring some pain.

It will change your daily routines.

It might make you complain.

You might have to change what you drink.

Maybe even change what you eat.

When you feel the urge to binge, my dear

try to stay away from sweets.

Water makes this change less crampy.

The more you drink, the easier it can be,

but this change will come whether you're ready or not.

Once your friend starts to visit, you will need to foresee

your life being prepared

to greet this new friend

anytime of the day, and

I recommend

that you start to see a doctor

working especially for you.

Take extra care of your hygiene;

be careful around boys, too

because this change makes a little girl

a woman whether she wants to be or not.

This change makes boys of all ages

want to talk to little girls a lot.

If you're not careful, this transformation can be

a blast from a baby

to a lady

overnight.

Chapter 7

"The Day Mr. Johnny Died"

Sunday mornings at our house were pretty routine. Up by six. Sunday school by nine. Morning worship at eleven. Family dinner and visits the remainder of the day, rain or shine. But this Sunday morning God had a different plan.

Ring, Ring, Ring! Grandma answers with jubilation in her hello. Mrs. Mary, our neighbor, was on the other end. I was sitting on the front room couch crash studying my Sunday school lesson, while Grandma talked, rather listened, on the phone. Grandma's silence was normal for certain phone conversations. She often preferred to be a good listener when women called, but today her silence was heavy. It weighed the air in the front room down. Grandma pulled the cord to her favorite corner of the couch, inches

away from me, and dropped like dead weight.

"Oh, no," she sighed. "I'll be right over," she

promised, and in a click, Grandma hurried out the door in

her duster, slippers, and tight curls.

Eight twenty-two had come, and I was slipping my

church shoes over my tights. The phone rang again.

"Hello," I answered.

"Izzie," Grandma was on the other end, "it's me,

Grandma."

"Yes, Ma'am."

"Mr. Johnny died this morning," Grandma confirmed

what I suspected since the first call. "I have to stay next

door and help Mary take care of things. While I'm over here, I need you to cook Sunday dinner today. Okay?"

"But I don't know how to cook Sunday dinner," I reminded her.

"It's okay. You know how to prep for it; you've done it for me a thousand times. So once I tell you the menu, I'll guide you through the rest. You can do it. I know you can. I can depend on you, right?"

"Yes, Ma'am."

Grandma spelled out a Sunday dinner menu of turnip greens with the bottoms, sweet potatoes, fried chicken, mashed potatoes, and made-from-scratch cornbread. I had my work cut out for me, literally.

I switched into my chill clothes, pressed play on my mixed gospel cd, and began cooking my first full Sunday dinner--alone. I started the turnip greens first because my mom and I had done the "hard part" the day before. Preparation, Grandma always said, makes performance less painful. I didn't have to call Grandma for this dish because I had watched her and my aunties prepare them since I was a little girl. As the greens slow-cooked in a covered pot, I began cleaning, seasoning, battering, and frying the dark meat in a cast iron pot. The grease got so hot at one point the fire alarm sent Grandma running back to the house to stop another Sunday tragedy.

"Izzie, she panicked. "You can't fry chicken that fast. We'll be eating pretty half-cooked chicken. Now, pour that grease out back and start over, but this time, keep the eye on medium."

"Yes, Ma'am."

Grandma feared she'd be running back and forth between both houses all day, so before she left she gave me a crash course on how to finish dinner. I had to skip worship service, a very rare occurrence, but I finished the entire dinner, including the cornbread, before the first family vehicle pulled up in front of the house.

"Mmmm, Izzie, you put yo' foot in these greens," Uncle Justin bragged.

"You sure you cooked all this by yoself?" Cousin Taylor playfully teased, smacking her lips on her second piece of chicken.

"Yes, I did," I replied. It was after four in the afternoon, and Grandma had not returned from Mr. Johnny and Mrs. Mary's house yet. I made sure to put her a plate in the microwave for later. Mrs. Mary's plate had already been sent over just in case Grandma decided Mrs. Mary needed to put something on her stomach. After slaving over my first meal, I was more excited to get off my feet than to try to eat. The laughter and happiness that replaced the heaviness in our home wasn't dampened because Mr. Johnny had died. Instead, the day Mr. Johnny died, a cook was born, and I became another person from my family to spread love and laughter through the comfort of Grandma's recipes.

****

Hidden Talents

You may not hit all your free throws

when you're out there on the court.

Your music notes may make the dogs bark at night

Your at-home practice may get cut short,

Your roses may not bloom

when you plant your first rose bush,

but you try anyway

Even if you need a push.

Your braids may be uneven.

Your experiments may explode.

Your first book may not sell well,

or it may on down the road.

Your healthy lifestyle change may not work

because you drank too much juice,

but I'm glad you tried anyway

even if you had a little boost.

We all have hidden talents

just waiting to be unveiled.

We a need cheering squad to keep us trying

no matter how many times we've failed.

What can you do?

You'll never know if there's no battle cry.

Yes, everyone has hidden talents,

Don't ever be afraid to just try.

Chapter 8

"Moana's Eyes"

Ms. Moana Mack, mack, mack. All dressed in black, black, black. With a golden zipper, zipper, zipper. All down her back, back, back. She asked her daddy, daddy, daddy. For a hundred dollar bill, bill, bill. He replied to her, her, her. For a hand job, I will, will, will. Moana Mack strutted into English class with a smile so bright that even the sun was jealous.

"What you smilin' for?" Laura asked.

Moana carefully positioned her leather jacket on the back of the desk in silence.

"Moana, Moana!" Laura shook Moana's shoulders with impatience. "Moana, girl you betta tell me what happened. What happened with you know who this weekend?"

"Girrrrl," Moana sang, "you know I don't kiss and tell."

"Good morning, class."

"Good morning."

Mrs. Peters was ready to guide us through another journey with Abigail and her religious traps, but today, by the glow in Moana's eyes, I could tell that she had some gossip from her weekend escapades that was much juicier than anything Arthur could create. I promise I was trying to be studious. I promise I had read the assigned pages the night before. I promise I was trying to mind my own business, but before I could write a response to the first guided question, it happened.

"Ahem. Ahem." Moana cleared her throat.

In an instant, Kenny and Walter had bum rushed Mrs. Peters's desk where she sat veiled with the current copy of *The Bolivar Commercial*. It was like every other student in the room knew what was happening, but me.

Three boys in the front-right corner raised their hoods over their heads with one hand and slipped their headphones over their ears with the other. Mrs. Peters screeched and giggled with Kenny and Walter.

"Mrs. Peters?"

"Yes, Yolanda."

"We all been reading together at home already. Is it okay if we work together to complete the questions?"

"I guess, Yolanda, but keep the volume down. Ok?"

"Yes, Ma'am. We will." A small group of students in the middle of the room formed a wall so fast James Bond couldn't infiltrate it. A mixed gender group in the front left corner formed a group. Students all over the room began to huddle and talk, snicker, gossip, chill, multitask.

In the back left corner, the area farthest from Mrs. Peters and the double agents, Moana and Laura turned their desks to face each other. It was coincidence that my desk was centrally located between the conversation.

"So, girl, what's up? Why you comin' up in here cheesin' and grinnin'? Somethin' happened. I know it. So spill it. SPILL IT, GIR--"

"SHHHhhh. Keep it down. Ion want Mrs. Nosey Peters gettin' in my business. We gotta whisper, and when

I tell y'all 'dis, you gotta promise me you ain't gon' tell no-bo-dy. I mean no-bo-dy."

"We promise," Laura answered for all four girls in our gossip-work group.

"Naaaaw," Moana sang. I need to hear it from all o' y'all." Moana started the covenant roll call. Lisa, you promise not to tell nobody?"

"I promise." Lisa sealed while linking pinkies with Moana.

"Deborah?"

"Girl, you know I got chu. Ain' gon' tell nobody. Ion never tell yo' secrets. How long we been friends?"

"I know, but what I'm 'bout to tell y'all if my mamma found out, y'all would be coming to my funeral next." Moana swiveled in her desk and squared up with me. Lips straight. Eyes frozen. Breath paused. Head tilted. "Izzie, you promise?"

"I promise." Our eyes locked. Our trust sealed. Our friendship changed forever.

Moana begins. "I ain't a virgin no more you know..."

Laura jokes, "Girl, that ain't know secret, we all know that."

"...but after 'da weekend I had, I ain't a whole lotta other thangs either."

"Jus' spill it. I'm tired of waitin'."

"Okay, okay. For the past week, I been feeling sick every mornin', so on Friday when I met up with my main man, we went and picked up a pregnancy test." The nagging quiet of her pause ate a hole in our need to know more.

"AND?" Laura asserted.

"and the test was positive. I was pregnant." I guess the rest of us were born yesterday because Deborah was the only person to pick up on Moana's full sentence. "What chu mean 'was'? How you "was" pregnant? You ain't pregnant no mo'?"

"No. Now just listen. Lemme finish before the bell rings. The first test came back positive, so we got another test, and I took it. That was positive, too. Soooo, like I was saying, my main man asked me to ride to his friend's house with him on Saturday. When we woke up, he had fixed me breakfast in bed--eggs, bacon just the way I like it, orange juice, waffles, strawberries, and apples. It was delicious." The smile on Moana's face contradicted the sadness in her eyes. No one else noticed it, but I did.

The rest of her weekend was something my sixteen-year-old virgin brain could not imagine.

Moana continued, "On the ride to his friend's house, he had the nerve to ask me if I really wanted to have the baby. Before I could even slap him for asking such a stupid question, he tried to question if the baby was even his. I told that fool that just cuz' I talk to other men, don't get it twisted. He is the only one of them I sleep with. I just talk to the other men for money, money that he gets to enjoy, too. Then, he tried to give me this sob story about how if I have this child, his child, he will have so much child support that he'll be living on the street or have to move back in with his momma. But I wouldn't havin' none of 'dat. So he got quiet until we made it to his friend's. As soon as we made it to his friend's house, they gave us drinks. I was like, "Whoa, Whoa, Whoa! Unh-unh, I ain't drankin' tonight. So Larry's girl brought me a glass of water. We laughed and played spades and dominoes for a minute. Then, Calvin pulled me outside. Girrrrl, we were about to go mud riding on four-wheelers. I didn't want to at first, cuz' I thought it wasn't safe for the baby, but Cal promised me that his other baby mommas always went mud-riding when they were pregnant. It was sooooo much fun, too. I couldn't believe it. It felt like going on a rollercoaster ride. By the time we finished mud-riding, I was so nasty and muddy that I had to take a shower before we went back home. We all went to shower. When I got out the shower, I was so dizzy and tired, so Cal laid me in Larry's bed. When I woke up, I couldn't do nothin' but scream to the top of my lungs. There was so much blood on the bed, my blood. I was having a miscarriage. I had a miscarriage. I-I lost my baby." Moana cradled her face in her hands as we sat in silence. When Cal came in the room, he didn't look surprised that I was bleeding, but he hugged me tight, and said, "Let's go home."

Laura couldn't be quiet any more. "So, you just went home? What? Are you crazy, Moana? You didn't tell your momma? You didn't go to the hospital? You couldn't call me? Are you still bleeding now? Why did you come to school today? You crazy? You shouldn't've come to school today."

"Well, I had to. If I would've stayed at home, I wouldn't have nowhere to go. Momma don't know what's goin' on, what I'm doin', or that I'm dating grown men, and after what Cal did on Saturday, I ain't foolin' wit' him no mo'. When we got back to Cal's house, he told me to put on something nice cuz' we had company comin' over. He told me he wanted me to be real nice to his company…"

Moana finished the rest of her weekend adventures. Her main man asked her to give his friends a happy time with her mouth. Her main man asked her to get on birth control. Her main man asked her to keep seeing her sugar daddies to keep their cash flow up. By the time her weekend story was coming to an end, I was certain that Moana's main man was not a man at all, but this Cal who Moana was hemorrhaging all of her morals and self-worth for, was the worst kind of monster--the kind that looks like your brother, father, or uncle.

"Did you do it?" Laura could not stand the suspense.

"What?"

"Did you do it? Did you do everything Cal wanted? Did you make your man proud?"

"Yep." Moana replied in a drowning whisper that was so unrecognizable all four of us had to look at Moana.

Moana's eyes were one minus one hundred thousand. Moana's eyes were a single parent holding the weight of the world on her back. Moana's eyes were trying to find land in the middle of the Bermuda Triangle. Moana's eyes were swimming in a sea of unanswered questions with no oxygen. Moana's eyes were a room the second the lights go out in the middle of a thunderstorm.

The bell rang. Moana stood up. "Remember, y'all, promises shared between friends…"

"...are kept 'til the end."

"Laura," Moana stopped in the hallway and struck a Tyra Banks's pose. "Let's go shopping this weekend for club outfits. I'm treatin'."

****

The Transaction

Momma, what was the price of milk when you were a little girl?

Ten cents, my child.

Momma, what was the price of bread when you were a little girl?

Five cents, my love.

Momma, what was the price of a dress when you were a little girl?

Fifteen cents, my baby.

Momma, what was the price of candy when you were a little girl?

One cent, my sweetie.

Momma, what was the price of gas when you were a little girl?

I'm not really sure, my child.

What about the price of a kiss from someone who cares for you?

Now, that, my child, was always free.

How about the price of time when someone really needs your help?

That should be free, too.

How much should you charge someone when they want a

different kind of love?

Now, honey, that is very complicated,

But let me be clear.

That kind of love between two people

Should never come with a price.

It's always priceless.

Why-why do you ask me such serious questions?

You are only sixteen.

Why do you want to know

such grown-up things?

Are you dating someone?

Do you have a crush?

Is some boy whispering sweet nothings in your ear

And making you blush?

Now it all makes sense, my child.

With all these questions.

I'm glad you trust me enough to talk,

But know there's no money in the world

that can pay for your love and respect, baby girl.

Your body's a temple.

Your heart is a throne.

Paper won't ever secure the crown on your head,

And any man that tries to make you believe that is wrong.

Prices of milk may go up.

Prices for gas will always change,

But when it comes to your self-worth, my queen,

I can't make this more plain.

Relationships are like transactions--

It's a give and take.

But when one person is taking more than he is giving,

the relationship is bound to break.

So one day when you're ready,

Find you a partner and work hard to do your part.

Just remember, my rare gem,

That when you're shopping for love, never put your self-

worth in the cart.

Chapter 9

"The Givers"

I lived fifty-two steps from Headstart. This is the
place where the seeds for my love of learning were
planted. Here, my first best friend, Forrest, and I sat at the
front of the mat during reading time. I was hypnotized by
the squeaky, scary, deep, and funny voices our teacher, Mrs.
Roberts, made while she read classics to us. I would go
home imitating her reading style to anybody who would
listen and even those who wouldn't.

I lived three-hundred seventy-six steps from Redde
Sea Elementary School, where my desire to learn was fed
and watered with almost the same twenty-five students from
Headstart. In first grade, my confidence was crushed when
for the first two nine weeks, I received an F in spelling on
my report card. I just knew I was going to fail first

grade. My teacher, Mrs. Stony noticed that I was not doing well, and instead of pouring more time into me, she ignored me. My grandma, of course, grabbed my hand, heart, and mind as we played games, developed songs just for me, and gave me the key to unlock the powers of the left-side of my brain, transforming my inferior frontal gyrus into a superior, powerful tool, which helped me begin to retain the spelling words. By the end of first grade I had all A's and a smile a mile long. I took that learning style of learning through games, songs, and association with me the rest of my life.

I lived forty steps from my Sunday School. At the age of ten, the primary class's Sunday school teacher was sick, so I was pulled out of the junior class to teach a lesson on David and Goliath. I fell in love with teaching. It was because of this experience that I discovered my gift for storytelling. Within a year, I advanced from being a substitute Sunday school teacher to an assistant Sunday school teacher to having my own primary Sunday school class. It was in this same church where my curiosity for a life outside of Redde Sea, a life beyond the Mississippi Delta was calling my name. At this Pilgrim's Rest church every year the community would come together and host the best Black History programs in the world. During the month of February, I would not want to be anywhere else except Pilgrim's Rest. We always had the premier politicians, social justice activists, and guest speakers from around the U.S. This was the first time I truly understood that it's not always what you know, but who you know that helps you get ahead in life. The youth, young adults, and community members of all ages and backgrounds would flock to the steps, pews, and choir stand of Pilgrim's Rest to be a part of these historic programs. As children and teens we got to cultivate and showcase our various talents in public speaking, singing, acting, videography, politics, collaboration, and a love for our heritage. These experiences were ingrained in my soul forever.

I lived sixteen miles from my middle school, and because Redde Sea Elementary School was permanently closed at the end of my fifth grade year, two-hundred seventy-eight other students and I had to be bussed to the next town in our district to continue our education, Riverside, Mississippi. This is the place where my interactions with others multiplied uncontrollably. No longer was I surrounded and influenced by the same people I knew since Headstart, but in Riverside Middle School I was exposed to students from approximately fifteen rural towns. The friends I grew up with were branching off to new friends, new experiences, and new decisions, and I was, too.

When I was in the sixth grade, we were given an invitation to join the middle and eventually high school marching band. This was my first step in the direction of opening a door to a brighter future for myself. When I started attending beginning band classes, our band director, Mr. Patrick Masters placed the alto saxophone in my hands, and I felt so light that the breath of a sleeping baby could send me floating into the clouds, just as long as the music I was creating with my lungs was flowing through the veins of that instrument. It was the gift of creativity that Mr. Masters and my six years of band gave me to take with me on my journey to womanhood. This gift of creativity is one of the traits that makes me see the world in semiquavers instead of wholes, in emotions instead of facts. It was during this magical transformation where I observed friends change their hairstyles, fashion, language, and values. I would often come home, sit on the couch with Grandma and talk to her about why the friends I used to have were gone. Grandma would remind me, "Izzie, some people are in our lives for a season, and some people are in our lives for a reason. No matter what happens, God has given us all a choice to learn and grow from the experiences, short or long." What I didn't realize at the time was that I was changing, too. However, as a teenager, I wasn't ready to understand what she meant by those words, but my lack of understanding never stopped her from consistently imparting that wisdom upon me.

I lived twenty-three miles from my high school, and there were many teachers, faculty, and peers who influenced my learning, but the two experiences that stood out the most were my mentor group and best friends Lisa and Aerial, and my eleventh grade English teacher Mrs. Catalyna Goad. My best friends became my high school family and support group. We taught each other how to study, manage time wisely, set and reach goals, and take risks. Together, there was nothing we couldn't conquer. We were ride or die for each other, and this mindset made teaching us a joy to all of our teachers. Our pact and tenacity also sparked many of our peers to follow suit, join our study groups, and turn in quality work. My high school learning couldn't have been more productive I thought, until we got a new eleventh grade English teacher, Mrs. Catalyna Goad.

Her teaching style was polar opposite of the traditional teacher. She would never answer a question for us. She provided a collection of resources and fostered collaboration in the class so that we could discover almost every answer we desired. She was enthusiastic. She was an Amazon woman, never afraid to challenge us academically, socially, and emotionally. One school day I walked into her class, and Mrs. Goad started placing a paper-bagged-wrapped book on all of our desks. Although I could not see the title or the book cover, I was engaged. The way she sold the book to us before she allowed us to tear the wrapping and open to the first page was better than any children's toy or latest shoe commercial I had ever seen. Mrs. Goad pitched, "This book shows how you can come from the bottom to the top, literally overnight. And, no," she emphasized, "the main character is not a rapper, or an athlete, or a singer, or an actor or actress. The main character is a young motherless, fatherless child who simply has the will to survive…" The will to survive. Those four words took my hand and walked me into another side of literature that no other teacher had trusted us, me to understand. Mrs. Goad was not like any other teacher, though. She guided us into the unfamiliar with confidence. I read my first college-level classic because of her. I attended my first musical because of her. I attended a variety of plays to supplement my learning because of her. I visited my first traveling museum because of her. I increased my wing span as a reader and writer because of her. Because of Mrs. Goad, I was able to not just peek through a window, open a door, imagine a life, or dream empty dreams. Because Mrs. Catalyna Goad was one of my eleventh and twelfth-grade teachers, I was able to walk proudly into any environment, awkwardness and all, and shine. Even when Mrs. Goad didn't believe in an initiative at school, she never let us see her skepticism. She exposed us to a world outside of the Delta through reading, field trips, summer programs, national competitions, and guest speakers. When I left her last class at the end of my senior year, I believed I could conquer the world, and I stepped on the college campus with a mission and a fire that no one could extinguish.

Those key interactions shaped my passion for living, growing, parenting, teaching, and becoming the woman I am today. No matter what pits, people, policies, programs, or pessimists were thrown my way, the church and schools in my community had ingrained within me a grit and love whose roots were as rich as the soil in the Mississippi Delta and whose reach was as long as the river that runs through it, through me. Because of them, I embrace change. Because of them, I teach the whole child. Because of them, I am an agent of change. Because of them, I always see hope--in every person--family, friends, students, colleagues, strangers--and now, me.

****

The River Runs Through Her

You can raise me well,

fully grounded to the core.

You can love my whole being,

but still one day, I'll have to soar.

You can give me a million reasons

to make your house my home,

but I still might have to fly

and try life on my own.

Don't fret your praying heart

I may stray for a while

You've nurtured my spiritual roots,

fed me the Word since I was a child.

Don't lose sleep at night

because God's got a plan

for me and my future

were born in his hands.

You surrounded me with a village

to show me how to grow.

That village gave me seeds to plant,

so now I must go

through the Desert of Zin

without my Moses

to the Promised Land

And therein

is where God shows his

bountiful power and purpose

for a girl becoming a woman

that the world does not prefer.

She may have made another place her home,

but she's fine because the river runs through her.

You gave me security.

You gave me heritage and pride.

You helped me unlock incredible gifts

that to the world, I could no longer hide.

You listened to my hopes and dreams,

and you sacrificed to keep them alive.

You watched me hit some bumps along the way,

but you still stood by my side.

You planted my roots

in grounds so fertile and rich.

You surrounded me with experiences

that helped me find my niche.

You secretly prayed and cried

that from my goals, I would not defer.

Your prayers were not unheard, my village

because a river runs through her.

Your tears were not in vain, my friends

because a river runs through her.

Your love was not in vain, my roots

because the river runs through her.

She will never forget.

Chapter 10

"Just Jump Already"

Rumors I heard as a child growing up about how Redde Sea got its name changed as I got older. In grade school, children used to say that our town got its name because a serial killer haunted the area killing people all over the Mississippi Delta, and he dumped their remains in the creek that runs like the letter c around our town. In middle school kids who didn't live in our town would tease us that our town was so dirty that all the rust from the junk in our homes and yards pooled into the creek every time it rained. By the time I was in high school, the rumor that dominated the classrooms was that Redde Sea was originally called Egypt, but during the great flood of 1927, hundreds of towns and cities were ruined by the Mississippi

River's floodwaters, but Egypt was not touched. People

who lived in our town during the time of the flood would

say, "It was like God himself had stretched out His hands

over the mighty Mississippi and protected this little

town. After that day, they officially changed the name to

Redde Sea, Mississippi. Even though the last rumor carried

a grain of truth, it was not until my Mississippi Studies

teacher taught a lesson on the geography of the Mississippi

Delta that we learned how Redde Sea got its name. The

torrential rains for months caused the Mississippi River to

swell. The swelling caused the levees to break. Every town

in the Mississippi Delta flooded, but Egypt, later named

Redde Sea, Mississippi, was untouched because of the

unique way the creek surrounded its land. At the same time,

algae mysteriously began to accumulate in the creek, forming a distinctive red tint that stayed in the waters for decades. Botanists who studied the phenomenon concluded that the algae were simply trying to survive.

Redde Sea, Mississippi had a lot of heritage. Every year, people traveled from near and far to witness the spectacular Black History programs, guest speakers, worship services, Christmas programs, parades, and other special events the Redde Sea community would put together. No child could ever say they did not know who they were or what their roots were living in Redde Sea, Mississippi. But under the same sun that shined so much love, community, and pride into our blood, the town of Redde Sea was dying.

Families were abandoning homes that once rang the cheerful sounds of children playing outside until after the streetlights came on. Holes appeared every five feet on the poorly-laid asphalt roads that connected driveways to driveways, families to families, churches to churches, and children to friends. When the only elementary school closed down, the first one of two gas stations relocated, too. By the time I was in high school, Redde Sea only had one general store. It was owned by an Asian family that had migrated to our area when it was booming with a bank, laundromat, clothing stores, thriving town hall, game room, and several Black and locally-owned restaurants. I knew my sweet town was not the same anymore, but it still had so much plain richness in its roots that it made me sick just to think about having to go away to college. By the time I was preparing to leave high school, I was faced with my own Red Sea. Should I go to a college that was close to home, or should I go to a college far away from home? No matter how many nights I prayed and pondered over this decision, I still could not make up my mind.

I had spent my entire life growing in the safety of the twelve streets of Redde Sea, Mississippi. I had never been kissed, never been missed, never been abandoned, never been abused. I had always felt love, family, friendships, hope, pride, compassion, patience, and empathy. I had never gone to a party by myself, never drank, never tried a cigarette, never worn make-up, or never taken a road trip with friends. Granddaddy had just bought me my first car. I had just received my first round of college acceptance letters and scholarships. I had just met a boy that I finally liked, and now I had to make a decision.

"Grandma, I'm going to store. I'll be back in a little bit. Do you need anything?"

"No, Izzie. I don't need anything. Just be careful out there, and don't stay gon' too long. Okay?"

"Yes, Ma'am." Grandma didn't know it, but in addition to the seven colleges I had already been accepted to with full-ride scholarships that my family knew about, I had also been accepted to a private Christian college called Holy Hill four hours away. The night before, I had packed everything I could in lawn-sized plastic garbage bags and placed them in the trunk of my car. I had strategically planned for Grandma to not need anything from the city that day because for days before, I secretly replenished all her

Ensures, insulin, Sunny D, needles, all my momma's popcorn, hot dogs, potato chips, eggs, sandwich meat, bread, and water. No one knew I was considering going to a college so far away from home. No one knew except me.

As I drove to the intersection where Redde Sea meets Highway 61, I looked to the left. That direction would take me back towards Riverside and to the grocery store, the place I told Grandma I was going. I looked to the right. That direction would take me down Highway 61 to Highway 6 to Highway 72 to Highway 78, and in four hours or less, I would be at the college I really wanted to attend-- Holy Hill. I would be at the place I knew I could start a new chapter in my life, meet a wider variety of people, and gain a wider variety of experiences. I could be in a new area where I could start all over where no one knows me except me. I could be myself and freely blossom into a baby bird finally learning how to fly.

The only thing that was holding me back was all the years of self-doubt and the fear of disappointing others who had sacrificed so much for me to make it this far. Turn left? Turn right? Turn left? Turn right? Beep. Beep. Beep. Beep! I jumped. I hadn't noticed a car pull up behind me. I had to make a choice now. I whipped the steering wheel to the right. That was the easiest without having to think about traffic coming both ways. I whipped the car to the right on a Friday morning, two days before I could officially move into Holy Hill's dorms. I had saved $6,000 from work study, and I knew that was enough to take care of myself for the first year of school because I was living on campus. I had already applied to jobs in the cities around Holy Hill. I was certain that I would have a job before my savings ran out. I was also sure that breaking the news to Grandma, and Granddaddy over the phone would be much easier than having to do it face-to-face.

As I drove down the highway, leaving the safety of a home I had known all of my life, I tried to concentrate on driving safely. The heartbeat of the Delta roads under my tires soon changed rhythm. Welcome to Lafayette County, the sign read. Before I could blink, I was at my resting point. My nerves had been screaming so loudly that did not realize that I had fifteen missed calls from the same number. 662-712-3456. The last missed call registered on my phone at 5:46 P.M. That was an hour ago. *I guess they have given up on me by now. I guess they found my letter I left in the kitchen. I guess they checked my closet and discovered that most of my clothes were gone. I guess they know now.* "Whew," I flicked the tears away that tried to change my mind. I did it. I took a chance. I was now one step closer to jumping into a new phase of my life, the phase where I just do what makes me happy.

As I lay in the bed of the hotel room, my mind wandered back to my little town after the great flood. Algae wanted to live there, businesses wanted to grow there, parents wanted to raise children there, pastors wanted to preach there, families wanted to reunite there, but I, I just wanted to leave there. Leave and make a better life for myself, so I could come back, get Momma, Grandma, and Granddaddy, and take care of them like they took care of me.

I left the safety of Redde Sea, a scared little girl trying to please everybody but herself. I crossed over into my freedom ready to try all of the things that my Redde-Sea mentality, deeply rooted in traditions, heritage, faith, and family, had been holding me back from being. I jumped out of the Redde Sea into a young lady, a growing woman that was learning, is still learning how to be unapologetically happy.

****

Life is about Taking Chances

Life is about taking chances,

Life is about taking risks.

Life is about never feeling regret

for the opportunities you've missed.

Life is about living in the present, and

leaving the past in your heart,

for living for the now will show you how

to embrace each day as your fresh start.

Life is what God gives your children

through the simple acts of your labor.

Because of His life, you're forgiven in spite

of your mistakes, God gives you his favor.

Life is about finding the little things

that keep a smile on your face.

just trust in His plan, put your burdens in His hands

He's already a hundred steps ahead in the race.

Life is about taking chances.

It's about taking the big dive.

Don't lose any sleep, or make promises you can't keep.

Just do you and be happy inside.

Life is not about living in the past

It's about living just for today.

With love in your foot, sometimes you need a little push,

for your past you can never replay.

So jump at every second you get

to live in the here and the now.

Don't cry over spilled milk; it's all in His will.

Nothing happens He doesn't allow.

So jump into living

Jump into being happy.

Jump into trying something new.

At the end of your life, you won't have ask why

Because you jumped at a chance for you.

Chapter 11

"My Biggest Fan"

She exited the car like Queen Elizabeth. Her smoothly, polished legs wrapped in flesh-colored silk. The finest fabrics graced her broad shoulders. Hand-strewn pearls adorned her neck. From where I stood in the procession, I only caught a glimpse of her grand entrance, but her escort made certain I saw them arrive.

"Izzie, Izzie!" She whisper-screamed from the steps of the auditorium. Her wave perfected with years of speaking to local strangers who barely paid her a nod. My arm dripping with sweat, I waved back ready to get out of the hot sun. The cap that accompanied this gown was only ornamental, for it did nothing to protect my weary head from the sun's wrath, yet, I waved back. I waved back in hopes that the wind I would trap in my sleeves would cool me down.

"Everyone take your places. It's time to begin." The professors were scurrying to lead us into the grand auditorium for our final walk as wanderers of the bardo. Once we exited these same grand doors, we would be a part of the working class, eventually.

These graduation ceremonies were not what my cheering squad were used to. Getting a degree from a private Christian college would not afford me the "yays, hoorays, and go Izzies" that ceremonies embraced back home. As I walked down the aisle with the rest of the graduates, I caught a glimpse of her. She had left her crown at home, for today was my day, but everyone she locked eyes with knew she was royalty.

"She has to be royalty," they whispered. "Why else would she speak to strangers as if we've known her for years? She has to be royalty."

As I marched closer to my seat, she snorted, trying to hold in her excitement, her pride, for today, her baby girl, her only child, was graduating from college.

"Good Morning," the mistress of ceremonies began. "Welcome to all of the families and friends of Holy Hill College graduating class of two thousand. Welcome to our board of trustees. Welcome to our prestigious alumni, but most importantly, welcome to the last day for the graduating class of two thousand. Roars of applause filled the room, and in an instant, as if someone had flipped a switch, the claps stopped. The graduation ceremonies proceeded as scheduled. At Holy Hill College, everything had been done in a smooth and orderly fashion. After all, that was the "Holy Hill Way." My back may have been seated to her, but she stayed at the front of mind.

I remember all the long nights she stayed up sewing outfits for me to wear in Black History programs, Christmas plays, school plays and awards ceremonies. I would watch her tired eyes light up whenever I wore her signature pieces with pride. Every year, we twinned it in mother-daughter pictures. Her shaky hands would always manage to smooth the strays in my newly plaited ponytails. Whenever I wanted fifty cents for a school snack, she simply rolled to the side, lifted the corner of her mattress, and unzipped her pocketbook. Long nights at football games were no match for her, for when the stands were no longer holding the fair-weather fans, my biggest fan was right there, holding the flash of her camera, waiting to get the perfect Kodak snapshot of her baby Izzie.

"Lewis Adam Geizer." The name reader was moving at a steady, tolerable pace. He was already in the Gs.

My mind took me back to the first day I saw her at her worst. Table shaking. Chairs toppling over. Her body was no longer under her control. To the six-year-old me, she appeared to move like a puppet tangled in the strings on the fingers of an angry puppet master. Her body slamming to the floor over and over, only to awaken after much-needed rest with no memory of the performance.

"Carla Denise Johnston. Patricia Anne Juneau. Zachary Donald Kepler..."

I can picture her like it was yesterday, sitting in the crowds at basketball games as I cheered on the lady wildcats, participated in school events, and sang in local programs. She would never have the experience of driving a vehicle herself, but for her baby girl, she read every book, took every note, and studied every driver just so she could have the honor of teaching me how to drive herself. She would coach me out to the countriest road and tell me step-by-step what she had studied in order to teach me how to drive. The faith and trust she had in me was unmatchable.

The day I graduated from high school, she spent that whole summer announcing it to all the land of Redde Sea that "her baby, Izrael Katrice Moses was going to college. I'm so proud of her," she would boast. I can't wait to see how God is gon' show up and show out for Izzie." And today, my biggest fan was getting to see me graduate from college.

I stood up with the fellow graduates in my row. We walked towards the steps to the right of the stage. *This is it. I am about to be a college graduate. I can't believe I made it.*

"Izrael Katrice Mo--,"

"Iiiiizzie!" she screamed and jumped to her feet. "Izzie, Momma so proud of you, Baby! You made it. You made it. You made it!" It was in this moment that the rest of the graduation guests' suspicions were confirmed. My biggest fan was royalty. In fact, she was more than royalty. She was a matriarch who had poured all she had into loving and nurturing her predecessor. She did not wear her crown today because it was not her greatest treasure. Her greatest treasure was walking across the stage wearing her Grandma's cross around her neck, her Granddaddy's handkerchief inside her gown, and her mother's crown upon her head. The day I graduated from Holy Hill College with a Bachelor's degree in secondary education, my biggest fan was the only one standing in a crowded auditorium, applauding as if she and I were the only ones in the room that mattered.

****

Daughter to Mother

Momma, what should I know before I go off to college?

"What you need to survive in this world, you can't find in book knowledge."

Momma, when will I know when I've found the right one?

"Slow down, Baby Girl, your life has just begun.

Momma, what can I be to make a lot of money?

"Baby, make yourself happy, and every day will be sunny."

Momma, is it better to be confident or is it better to be humble?

"Baby, be who you are because God makes a victory out of a mumble."

Momma, what if praying is not working for my pain?

"Then, therapy's better than dying inside from the

unstoppable rain."

Momma, what will I do when my friends move away?

"You'll move on with your life; you might see them again

someday."

Momma, why am I so different; why is it hard to make

friends?

"Stop trying to mix what God never meant to be a blend."

Momma, do you judge me for my choices, or love me for

who I am ?

"You can be living under the ground with moles, and I'll

still be your biggest fan?"

Momma, how can I hold my head so high when the world keeps pushing me down?

"Pray about it, go to sleep, then wake up, and fix your crown."

Momma, how do I keep moving up in life, when others' actions cause bad blood?

"Keep your distance, keep your vision, and keep killing them with love."

Momma, what can you suggest I do when my brain and heart are in a living grave?

"Go for a walk, take a vacation, write your thoughts on paper, and through it all, be brave."

Momma, if I'm having a bad hair day, what's a girl to do?

"Baby, our strands are resilient, they're a part of what makes us brilliant, so keep it clean, and just be your beautiful you."

Momma, how do I pick up the pieces when someone breaks my heart?

"Protect your self-respect before letting someone affect your peace. You've got this; you're smart."

Momma, who do I lean on when it feels like no one understands?

"Whether I'm here or I'm not, God is always on watch, and I'll always be your biggest fan."

Chapter 12

"Broken Compass"

The outside of 524 Lenore Street wore her refreshing coat of nature with grace. Her eyes were abnormally bright. Her veins pumped warmth into the hearts of everyone who entered her arms. She protected us all from floating adrift.

Within the walls of 524 Lenore Street, things were slowly falling apart. The captain and co-captain of this great ship were sailing their last voyages before our eyes, and many of us, especially the grandkids had just learned to cast our sails. I had a hull. I had a keel. I had a stern with a battered rudder. I had an anchor that I didn't quite know for myself, but the day had come for all of us to cast our own sails.

My dear captain took her swim first, deep-sea diving was her favorite. She was ready to get her water wings, but right before she took the plunge, she placed in my palms her special compass. "I won't need this anymore, Izzie," she spoke softly. Her touch, even more delicate than the air. "You take this compass to help guide you on your new journey, and always remember the magnetic fields that will make it work." Before she jumped in, I didn't want to miss the last time I would see her face-to-face, so I didn't look at the compass she gave me until after her co-captain took his final swim, too.

We drifted together as a crew without our leaders for as long as we could, but soon we all had to cast our own sails, take on new directions, navigate the seas the best we knew how. Roger, Miller,

Deandre, and Tara drifted southwest towards the Texas

borders. Allison floated towards the Atlantic Ocean.

Destiny, Samantha, Beneatha, Willie, Solomon, and

Shameka quickly found land where the ground freezes

often. Maymie, Martin, Terrell, and Pierre became sea

gypsies, but E.J., Justice, and I attached our lines to the bow

of Lenore's unmanned ship. I casted my anchor before it

was time, afraid I would lose my way, and not find the road

back home.

Still close to home, I felt like I was thriving, sailing

my own way. It was not until I drifted into the storms of

life that the darkness tried to consume my light. When the

winds started blowing, I gripped the helm of my boat, trying

to keep control. No matter how tightly I held on, I was

tossed to and fro. I managed to close my sails, and hold on for dear life, but when the storms subsided, I was totally lost. With my head lowered in despair, I thanked God for his mercy and laid eyes on the compass my captain left in my care. This had to be a sign that I was not lost at all because this compass could take me wherever I needed to go. I steadied my captain's compass in my hand, but for some reason, it would not work. I tapped it, shook it, even took it apart and put it back together the way my captain had shown me so many times before, but it still would not work.

I'm lost. I'm lost. I give up. I can't do this anymore. "If anybody can hear me, I give up!" I screamed to the top of my lungs. I dropped to my knees. The weight of my sins almost sending me overboard. I lifted my head and hands to the sky. "I. GIVE. UP!" In that moment, the needle in my captain's compass moved like it was possessed. I fixed my eyes on that compass every morning, every break, every night before I closed my eyes to rest, until its needle showed me the way. From the reaction of the compass, I knew someone could hear me, even when I felt so alone, so I just kept talking to the person who was guiding the compass until I could operate my sails through any storm. I just kept talking to the one guiding the compass until I knew how to navigate those unpredictable waters depending solely on the magnetic fields.

For many years, I thought the compass I had inherited from my captain was broken, useless, silly. I only carried it with me because I believed that whether broken or not the compass would keep me safe.

It was not until many years later that I realized that it was not the compass my captain gave me that was keeping me going in the right direction. It was her faith in the magnetic field that she would never see with human eyes that kept her compass working, kept her family bonding, and kept her ship sailing the right way. And now my faith would continue to allow the compass to do the same for me. No matter which way the wind blew, the compass my captain left me would help me adjust my sails.

****

I Can't Take You with Me

On Sunday, I'm taking you to the grocery store,

so you can learn how to budget.

I want you to be able to shop one day on your own

and make the best judgements,

for whether you believe it or not,

the future you won't always foresee

cause life can throw you curveballs,

and I have to set you free.

Tomorrow we're going to the beauty shop

to get your hair done.

I want you to know how to groom yourself nicely

while you're still young.

Now, don't get me wrong: your natural beauty is just fine,

but sometimes a lady likes a different look.

So when you get the urge to color, curl, cover, or cut your

hair,

an appointment, you'll know how to book.

On Wednesday, I'm taking you to Bible class,'

so you can know the Word for yourself.

Study it everyday and consistently pray,

so from this world you will accept nothing less.

On Friday, I'm taking you bowling,

But not before we do all our chores.

Because play rarely comes before work, my dear.

In life you have to take care of what's yours.

On Saturday, I'm taking you to a museum

to see other cultures in a different light.

Because one day you'll leave the familiars you've known,

and your lifestyle won't always be right.

But today, I'm taking you to school

because an education will often guarantee

that you can go out into the world and rock it like a smart

girl,

because one day I'll be gone, and I can't take you with me.

Chapter 13

"Twenty-five"

Today I turned twenty-five. My husband has planned a dinner for me at my favorite Mexican restaurant, and all our close friends and family will meet us there to celebrate another glorious year on this earth for me. The sun's rays provide the perfect lighting for an I-woke-up-like-this selfie. The silence in the background tells me that either Jordan has the baby back asleep or the sleep gods are smiling down on this birthday mom.

Knock! Knock! Knock! My husband peeks through the doorway to see if I was actually awake. "Happy birthday to ya!" Clap. "Happy birthday to ya!" Clap. "Happy birirthdaaay." Clap. He sings in his best Stevie voice. "Happy birthday to ya!" Clap. "Happy birthday to ya!" Clap. "Happy birirthdaaay." Clap. Jordan's hounddog melody coupled with his senior citizen Dru Hill dance moves put a light in my eyes that Apollo would envy. "Happy birthday, Baby. Jordan's kiss sealed the first of many presents of love and affection he had planned for my special day. I was ready to relax and laugh with the people who meant so much to me. My sister-in-laws were coming over. My mom was here. My best friends had driven miles just to help me celebrate being twenty-five, a fine new mom, and a boss wife. I'm twenty-five. What more could a woman ask for? Educated? Check. Married? Check. Family? Check. Happy? Check, check.

By 8:49, Lisa and Ariel were already banging on the front door.

"Izzie! Open the door, girl. You ready to go get pampered?" Ariel's cheerful tone increased my excitement meter to a thousand."

"Hey, y'all," I greeted my friends with bear hugs.

"Hey, Izzie," Ariel smiled.

"Heeey, Izzie," Lisa shrieked, "Happy birthday."

"Thanks."

"Happy birthday, Izzie," Ariel added, "Now go take that scarf off your head and let's go. We can't be late for our spa day."

"Yeah, girl. You got fifteen minutes before we leave you," Lisa teased.

"Okay, okay. I'm going. I'll be ready in five." I scurried to my room, combed out my wrapped hair, kissed both my babies goodbye for a while, and hurried out the door with my two best friends for some much needed relaxation.

"So, Izzie," Lisa said, "What's it feel like to be twenty-five?"

"I don't know," I shrugged. "I don't know."

"Whatchu mean, I don't know?" Ariel demanded.

"I mean, I don't know. I don't feel like twenty-five. I tell you that."

"Mmm Hmm," Ariel could sense something was off, but she let me slide because it was my birthday.

The ride to the spa was only seven minutes away according to GPS, but the awkwardness of our conversation made it seem more like seventy. I was relieved when they called our names for our massages and facials. This location could not accommodate three people in one room at the same time, so Lisa had booked us all separate rooms.

Just as I'm switching my phone to silent mode, I get a new message. I read it. I wish I hadn't.

I'm not gonna respond.

Soft lights, $5 an hour. Heated table, $10 an hour. Instrumental jazz in the background, $3 an hour. Fresh crisp linens to shield my skin, $2 an hour. Time and patience of a skilled masseuse minding her own business, $65 an hour. Silence and alone-time for an hour on your birthday, priceless. The masseuse's hands had found their rhythm.

"So, what brings you in to us today?" the masseuse just had to talk. "I mean, what areas would you like me to spend more time on--your feet, shoulders, neck, back--just let me know."

"My back. I mean I just had a baby five months ago, and my back, especially my lower back just hadn't snapped back yet."

"Okay," she says. "Just relax your mind, close your eyes, and I'll take care of the rest."

That is just what I was planning to do. My body switched to autopilot, but my mind, my mind just would not wind down. I'm twenty-five today, twenty-five, but deep down I feel like a twenty-five pennies rattling around in a piggy bank, and somebody's itching to break me open. Why does Jordan have to ruin everything? I won't let him, though 'cuz it's my birthday. Today I'm twenty-five, and all my closest friends and family will help me celebrate this special day at my favorite Mexican restaurant. I will smile and laugh and joke and party like I just won the lottery. Today is my birthday, and I deserve to be happy.

"All done," the masseuse walked towards the door. "Take your time getting dressed; I'll meet you in the hallway when you're ready."

I thanked her, got dressed, and tipped her. Lisa, Ariel, and I shared a huge sigh of thanks as we headed back to my house. "I really needed that me-time. Thank you so much. I mean it. You took off work and drove three hours just for me. Thank you both so much."

"Izzie, you know we gotchu," Lisa winked.

"Yeah, Izzie, we always gotchu." Ariel agreed.

I walked in the door, and in the process of reaching for my baby from the arms of my husband, Jordan diverts baby August to the arms of Lisa.

Snatching me by my elbow, he asserted, "We need to talk--now!"

"Okaaay?" I released my arm from his grip and followed him to our bedroom. The door closed. *What is wrong with him?*

"With little hesitation, Jordan began. "What is wrong with you, Izzie? Why can'tchu jus' do what you're supposed to do?"

"I don--. What are you tal--?"

"How many times do I have to tell you to clean this house before company comes over? I know it's your birthday and all, but you knew we were having people over weeks ago, so you should have started cleaning this house a little bit at a time earlier this week. There is no excuse for how nasty this house is...how nasty you are." Jordan's mouth was out of control.

"but I didn--, you need to--"

"And another thing," he continued, "what kind of a woman, what kind of a mother would go for days with her baby living in a house where the clothes aren't put up, the dishes are piling up, everything is just a mess. You're a mess. You gotta get it together, or stop inviting people over here altogether." Jordan's words whipped the eight-year-old me crouched in the corner in fear when I disappointed my granddaddy. Jordan's words lashed the thirteen-year-old me enduring months of teasing from a boy I rejected. Jordan's words struck the sixteen-year-old me who never felt smart enough, pretty enough, or good enough to even love myself.

The more Jordan huffed and puffed, the more I was building a brick wall around my mind, my heart. The whole time I was fighting to protect the pieces of me that were taking the most blows, my bullet-proof vest was weakening. The bullets that spewed from his lips had a target on the part of me that whispered, "You can do it" when all the doors are closed. His words sprayed insults at me that silenced the inner twenty-five-year-old me down to a bounced check.

Why wasn't I woman enough to stand up to Jordan? Why was I letting him treat me like this? Why couldn't he see the pain he was causing? Why wasn't I strong enough to shut him up? I'm a grown woman after all. I am a mother. I have my master's degree in psychology. I'm somebody's wife. I'm a twenty-five-year-old grown woman, and it's my birthday today. My husband has planned a dinner for me at my favorite Mexican restaurant, and all our close friends and family will meet us there to celebrate me living one more glorious year on this earth, but in this moment

I feel like a bright yellow balloon,

floating so high in the sky

that you would have to

squint your eyes

to see

it.

****

Priorities

Learning to know who you are is

One of the biggest battles you'll have to face.

Vowing to not forget your worth is not as

Easy as one might think to embrace

Your worth, your smile, your voice, your

Own, your style, your

Uniqueness, your flaws, your crown, your throne

because

Real friends, real family, real love, real life

Stand beside you through it all,

Every time the world tries to downsize your

Laugh, your words, your voice, your worth,

For the world

Fears your power and purpose on this earth.

Instead of hiding in the sand

Raise your head and be heard

Stand up for yourself and

Tell yourself these queen words

You're the bomb, you should always be

On top of the world

Unmovable, your name on a marquee

Ask to please no one else before you make yourself

smile

Release life's hold on your actions

Expect pushback for a while

Allow you to be you

Leave your doubts at the door

Welcome the

Awesomeness that holds hands with

Your awkwardness, and your

Self-love will grow stronger, for sure.

Each day that you breathe let

No one force you to live in-between what

Others want you to be, and

Unleash your inner queen

Grab your crown

Hang on for the reign because your priorities are in

order--You're number one.

Chapter 14

"The Ride Home"

Maybe it was because she was different.

Maybe it was because she was outspoken.

Maybe it was because she loved the skin she was in.

Maybe it was because she was in love, and it showed through her smile, the rise and fall of her heart as she breathed throughout the day.

I will never know the real reason for what they did to her, but what I do remember is the ride home.

I was the youngest lady in the car of the four of us carpooling back and forth for a month to a training at a university. Before this training, we had all only breathed the same oxygen at district-mandated professional developments.

"Did y'all see what Laci had on today?"

"I sure did. She looked like the hungry, hungry hippo." Explosions of laughter smothered the Christian music playing in the background.

Today, it was my turn to ride shotgun. Because these three "30-40-year-old ladies" had made it their priority to make Laci the focus of their conversations since the start of our summer training, I wanted to scream. Instead of screaming, I turned my head toward the passenger window to hide the wrinkles their words and actions were painting on my forehead and splashing in the angles of my eyes.

Our driver for the week, the preacher's wife, continued, "Why do y'all think she dresses like that and talks so much?"

"I don't know," one of the ladies from the back replied, "but someone should tell her to stop talking so much. I mean, especially to me. Hmph. She must think I like her or something?"

"I know right. Does she know that her lifestyle in itself is a sin, and no matter how friendly she is, how much good she does for others, she is still going to hell?

"What?!" I intervened. "What are you talking about? What do you mean by that statement? Why are y'all talking about Laci like that?"

The lady who overcompensates her beauty with colors from the rainbow answerered first. "You know why. She is annoying, and she thinks she knows everything. She talks too much, and parades her sexuality around like it's a badge of honor."

"Mmm Hmm," the other two ladies sang in unison.

"And it's not. Every time she tries to talk to us...me, what I really want to tell her is SHUT UP! I don't like you. I don't agree with your lifestyle. I don't like you. Don't talk to me."

"Well, why do y'all fake and laugh and talk to her all the time? Why don't you just keep your distance? Don't you think what you're doing is wrong? You're being hypocrites."

"What!" Their flummoxed response changed the direction of the conversation.

"Yes, you're all hypocrites."

"Noooo. We're not hypocrites. Why do you think we're hypocrites?"

"You're hypocrites because you all boast and brag about how much you love the Lord, but in the same day, the same ride, the same breath, you tear down a person you barely know who God created. But you "love" the Lord. How is that? I've been listening to y'all this whole ride home condemn Laci to hell, and for what? How can you call yourselves Christians if you constantly bash other people? You're just mean girls dressed in choir robes. Don't think that just because you're saved, you can't go to hell."

"We can't. Once saved, always saved. Jesus says: I give them eternal life, and they shall never perish; no one can snatch them out of my hand. My Father, who has given them to me, is greater than all; no one can snatch them out of my Father's hand. I and the Father are one.' The forgiveness of God through Christ is sufficient to cover all of our sins -- past, present, and future. There is nothing a person can do that God cannot forgive." The minions in the backseat shook their heads in agreement.

The mere fact that Reverend Stone's wife attempted to use Bible scripture to convince me that saved people get unlimited free passes to willingly mistreat those who live different lifestyles from them, and that all self-professed Christians/churchgoers would have eternal life in the eyes of God was cute, but I was not converting.

My top teeth met my bottom teeth with fury, skating back and forth as I searched the empty fields we passed to find the best words to let them know how I felt.

Remember, Izrael, you're not like them. You grew up differently. You are a different race. You have a different culture. You obviously have different values. Relax. relax. Maybe this conversation is best left here. Mayb--.

"Look!" I commanded, "I am a child of God, too. I may not be able to repeat scripture like a robot. I may not be an ordained minister. I may not attend church every Sunday, but I am a child of God, just like you and you and you. And if right now, right now, I didn't have this tiny ounce of Faith that I have in me right now, if I had not been saved already, listening to you guys use your Christianity as armour to protect you from your disgusting hatred, racism, prejudices, and whatever else you're hiding behind those smiles, I would never even give God a chance."

"Now, you just wait one min--"

No, you wait. We should be treating people the way we want to be treated despite their lifestyles. That won't ever mean that treating someone with kindness is you agreeing to or supporting their lifestyles. It just means that you love and respect them as a human, a child of God, too. That's sad how y'all are treating Laci, and she has no clue."

One lonely tear held on for dear life as I turned my head to finish the ride home in silence. The teardrop soon turned into a steady leak as I heard nothing from my carpoolmates the rest of the ride home either.

When we pulled into the Circle K parking lot, I gathered my bag from the trunk and beelined it to my car. *Should I tell Laci? Should I just leave it alone? Should I drive myself for the remainder of the training? Should I just suck it up and move on?* So many decisions raced through my strained head that I knew making a decision at that moment would not be wise. I cranked my truck, backed out of the parking space, and

headed home to hug my babies.

God,

It's me, Izrael.

Say no more, my child, I have the answer. "...Whoever does

not practice righteousness is not of God, nor is he who does

not love his brother. (1 John 3:10)

****

The Sunday School Lesson

The writing's in the dust,

not on the wall.

Because if it was on the wall then

it would be clear as acne

that God loves everyone,

Even those whose sins ooze white pulse and leave an ugly

scar behind.

The writing's in the dust,

not in the news.

Because if it was in the news,

the whole world would be the judge

 and the jury with circumstantial evidence.

How can the evidence of a pig in the sky prove the pig can

fly?

How can going to church prove you believe in God?

How can getting baptized prove you will go to Heaven?

How can catching someone in the act prove they are a

habitual adulterer?

How can he without sin cast the first stone, Mrs. Stone?

How can smiling in the face of a person you don't like make

you a good person?

How can you truly trust yourself if you can't show who you

really are when it matters most?

Is the writing in the dust for you,

or are you walking away with the crowd?

Made in United States
North Haven, CT
01 December 2022

27647041R00095